W9-BKK-023

NOTHING FITS A
DINOSAUR

For the Mommasauruses and Daddysauruses

who kept us from extinction

SIMON SPOTLIGHT
An imprint of Simon & Schuster Children's Publishing Division
1230 Avenue of the Americas, New York, New York 10020
This Simon Spotlight edition August 2021
Text and illustrations copyright © 2021 by Jonathan Fenske
SIMON SPOTLIGHT, READY-TO-READ, and colophon are registered
trademarks of Simon & Schuster, Inc.
For information about special discounts for bulk purchases, please contact
Simon & Schuster Special Sales at 1-866-506-1949
or business@simonandschuster.com.
Manufactured in the United States of America 0222 LAK
2 4 6 8 10 9 7 5 3
Library of Congress Cataloging-in-Publication Data
Names: Fenske, Jonathan, author, illustrator.
Title: Nothing fits a dinosaur / by Jonathan Fenske.
Description: Simon Spotlight edition. | New York: Simon Spotlight, 2021. |
Series: Ready-to-reads. Level 1 | Audience: Ages 4–6.
Summary: After being told no drama and to put on his pajamas, the dinosaur is
unimpressed and romps around the house undressed since human clothes are
much too small for such a mighty dinosaur.
Identifiers: LCCN 2021003394 | ISBN 9781665900652 (hardcover) | ISBN 9781665900645
(paperback) | ISBN 9781665900669 (ebook)
Subjects: CYAC: Stories in rhyme. | Clothing and dress—Fiction. | Dinosaurs—Fiction. |
Bedtime—Fiction. | Humorous stories.
Classification: LCC PZ8.3.F3664 No 2021 | DDC [E]—dc23
LC record available at https://lccn.loc.gov/2021003394

NOTHING FITS A
DINOSAUR

BY JONATHAN FENSKE

Ready-to-Read

Simon Spotlight

New York   London   Toronto   Sydney   New Delhi

"No more playtime,"
says my momma.

"Take a bath.
Put on pajamas.

And please, tonight,
no dino drama."

The bath is fun!

I romp and stomp

inside my tiny
bathroom swamp.

But finding jammies
is a chore
when nothing fits a dinosaur!

These claws would tear
a shirt in two.

This cozy quilt
will have to do.

And pants cannot
contain these thighs.

Two sleeping bags
are more my size.

What kind of socks
will warm these toes?

Some pillowcases,
I suppose!

Why stop there?
My feet could use
a decent pair
of stomping
shoes!

But these
will barely fit a mouse!

—MINE!

So let these buckets
shake the house!

And now my noggin
needs a hat.

A lampshade will take care of that.

Did I forget
my underwear?

I have a tail.

I hang it there.

Now I am such
a silly sight.

A dressed-up dino
is not right.

These clothes shall feel
my DINO-MIGHT!

I shed them with
a mega-roar!

I kick them all
across the floor!

No shirt.

No pants.

No socks.

No shoes.

No hat.

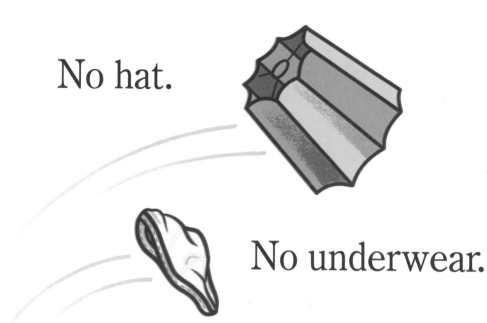

No underwear.

I choose
to dress in NOTHING!

Look at me!
NOTHING fits me
perfectly.

Watch me romp

and stomp

and roar!

A naked,
happy
dinosaur!

I run wild,
and I run free!

As bare as dinosaurs
should be . . .

... till Mommasaurus
roars at me:

"NO MORE PLAYTIME! THAT IS IT!"

I better find some
clothes that fit.